Valentine:
An Alien Scifi Romance

DEMELZA CARLTON

ONE

"You really should consider putting in a request for a replacement heart. I could file it for you, marked as urgent…but you'd have to transfer to the *Genesis* for the procedure. Our medbay here on the *Magellan* malfunctions so often, it's only a matter of time before it pronounces someone dead while their heart's still beating."

Valentine forced himself to smile at Maia, despite the dread squeezing his heart. She held his fate and his secret in her hands. He could only hope she wasn't the sort to betray or blackmail him over it. Not unless his life depended on it – if she was as good a medic as her misguided thoroughness indicated, she would have no qualms about revealing his secret to save his life. He had to hope it never came to that. "This heart belongs to my wife, Anna. I'm not sure if she'd forgive me if I replaced it, even with a better model. Besides, it's kept beating this long – I'm sure it can wait until after the war is over. We're short on techs as it is – the *Magellan* needs me."

As if the *Magellan* had heard him, the

alarm blared into life, summoning all available crew to battle stations.

"If I don't get down to Engineering, the ship will probably fall apart. You get into one of the port side lifepods — remember I haven't had a chance to fix the starboard ones yet. Can't have the ship's only medic hurt by a malfunction." He saluted her and set off down the corridor.

Maia called after him, "I remember. You get your arse down to Engineering, and keep us all safe."

Valentine sighed. That's what this whole war was about — keeping everyone safe from the aliens out there that had invaded the Altan system. He'd never expected it would also mean keeping everyone safe from space itself in a ship that threatened to break down at least a dozen times a day. If he had his way, the *Magellan* would have been turned into scrap metal a long time ago.

Just as long as they were all safely disembarked when it happened.

"There you are. Thank the stars – I thought I'd have to keep this ship running by myself!" Baris exclaimed as Valentine jogged into Engineering.

"As if I could sleep soundly in my bunk, knowing you have sole responsibility for the whole ship's safety," Valentine joked.

Baris glanced up at the ceiling before saying in a hushed whisper, "If it were left up to the ship, she would kill us all in our sleep. I pray the war ends soon, before she gets that chance." For what was likely the hundredth time that day, Baris's hands curled into horns to ward off any bad luck the evil eyes of the *Magellan* might wish upon him.

Valentine wasn't as superstitious as Baris, but he had to admit sometimes he wondered if luck was all that held the *Magellan* together. Good luck, not bad.

Because good luck had saved his wife Anna when the Titan terrorists attacked her lab on Elysium, and good luck would keep them both safe until he returned home to her. He had to believe it. Or what was he fighting for?

The comm on the wall buzzed. "Bridge to Engineering, come in?" The words were barely audible through the static. The comm system needed repairs as much as anything else on this ship, but they wouldn't get time today.

Baris was closer. "This is Engineering."

Valentine prayed that they needed a repairman to fix something on the bridge. A sparking console, perhaps.

Of course, he wasn't that lucky.

"Bring the reactor up to full capacity. I want all available power diverted to the engines, immediately."

Baris's mouth dropped open. To be fair, so did Valentine's. Running the reactor at more than half capacity risked blowing up the ship and anything in that sector of space. Full capacity could kill them all.

Valentine recovered his voice first. "Uh, Bridge, you realise the reactor can't sustain that level of power output. The magnetic containment field can't hold it for long, and stuff starts to melt. At best, we can give you fifteen, maybe twenty minutes at maximum power, before we have to vent at least half the plasma."

There was a pause, followed by, "Acknowledged, but the order stands. Give the engines as much juice as you can, and when you vent the plasma, try to send it in the same direction as the engines are pointing. Twenty minutes will have to be enough. Bridge out."

Baris stared at Valentine, his thoughts adding up the information at the same time.

"Whatever's out there, we're running from it."

"It must be bad, if we're risking a reactor overload to do it."

Valentine swallowed. "Well, if we can't outrun it…a reactor overload's a better way to go than slowly suffocating in space. At least it's pretty much instantaneous."

Baris managed a sickly smile. "If it's all the same to you, I'd rather not die today, or overload the reactor. Let's get this thing fuelled up. The sooner we do, the sooner we can vent it."

"Agreed."

Valentine increased the fuel flow steadily, never taking his eyes off the screen, while he knew Baris watched the control console for warning lights with equal intensity. With a ship as old as the *Magellan*, it wasn't a matter of if a warning appeared, as when it would.

"Right, that's the fuel going in. Setting

up the power diversion now," Valentine said, more to himself than anything else, but out of the corner of his eye, he saw Baris nod.

No warnings yet.

"All spare power diverted to the engines, with the exception of auxiliary battery reserves," Valentine said. The fuel was steadily trickling into the reactor, so he had a minute to satisfy his curiosity. "Want to see whatever it is we're running from?"

"Stars, yes," Baris said.

Valentine pulled up the external sensors, scanning through the feeds, but all he saw were…rocks. Floating in the black. "We're in an asteroid field. Plenty of rocks, but there's no one out here but us."

Baris frowned. "Sensors must have picked up something, if we're risking the reactor to run from it. Not to mention venting precious fuel. Maybe it's stealthed so we can't see it, or hiding behind one of the rocks."

Valentine saw a flash of light, an instant before something slammed into the ship, sending them sprawling.

"Something's out there, and it's shooting at us!" Baris cried, his eyes wide with fright.

"Run away, run away," Valentine muttered to himself, his eyes darting from the reactor to the control board to his display. The vacuum chamber was full, magnetic containment was holding, and the temperature had begun to rise. Yep, the engines were definitely accelerating — in an old ship like the *Magellan*, you could feel the g-force, even through the artificial gravity. Not like the *Genesis*.

Another impact shook the ship, sending Valentine to his knees. Whatever was firing on them, it was keeping up. At this rate, any extra power from the reactor would be too little, too late.

A third shot cannoned into the ship. Valentine hung on to the bulkhead, barely managing to stay on his feet, but Baris wasn't so lucky, slamming into the reactor wall.

A new alarm began blaring. Valentine's eyes darted to the control board, but none of the reactor warning lights glowed red yet.

"Attention all crew. Abandon ship.

Get to an escape pod and abandon ship. Attention all crew…"

It was a recorded message, but something in the emotionless tone chilled Valentine more than a human voice might have. Had their enemy taken out the bridge, and now they were drifting in space, with no one at the helm?

They had to shut the engines down, and the reactor. If they didn't, it wouldn't matter how many people made it into escape pods – the pods wouldn't survive the fusion bomb the ship would become.

"Baris! Help me shut this down." When he didn't receive a response, Valentine yelled, "Baris!"

Baris slid down the side of the reactor and lay on the floor, unmoving.

"Stars," Valentine swore. He checked Baris was breathing – he was – but his hands came away bloodied. A quick search revealed a head wound and burns from where Baris's back had been against the reactor wall too long.

Valentine felt gravity slipping, and activated the magnetic field on his boots, anchoring himself to the ground. Baris floated up, like something out of an occult horror movie. Valentine grabbed Baris and launched them both toward the nearest escape pod. He shoved his unconscious colleague inside, set the stasis field to activate as soon as the pod was clear of the ship, and closed the doors. "See you in salvage," he said as the escape pod launched.

A new alarm sounded, but Valentine

recognised this screech — it was the temperature sensor on the reactor heat exchanger. Time to shut it down. Valentine reached for the controls. He considered only venting half the fuel, as ordered, then thought better of it. If there was no one to monitor the ancient reactor, even at half power, it was likely to do something disastrous. Better to vent the whole vacuum chamber.

The computer asked for extra verification codes — this was something you only did in emergencies, after all — and Valentine entered them. On second thought, he should activate the extra coolant dump, too, just in case. As his hands touched the controls, lightning arced across the board, seizing him in its relentless grip so he couldn't break free.

An eternity passed, the current burning through his very bones, before Valentine toppled over, away from the console. Everything ached, but the pain in his chest was the worst. If Maia were here, she'd have her emergency, he thought, as the throbbing ache moved down his arm and into his jaw. This must be what a heart attack felt like.

"Attention all crew. Abandon ship. Get to an escape pod and abandon ship…"

Valentine managed a stiff nod. Yes, he'd obey that order now. Because if he could make it into stasis, whoever revived him could deal with the heart attack and replace whatever parts of him they wanted. Maybe Maia.

Valentine swam through the reactor

room, headed for the nearest escape pod. He dived inside, kicking the door controls with his foot so they closed behind him.

"Stasis will engage in five…four…

Oh, but Anna wouldn't be happy. His heart belonged to Anna.

"Three…two…"

He'd get her a new one. She deserved a new one that beat only for her and never, ever threatened to give up.

"One…zero."

As long as she was safe. He had to believe she was safe, and that he'd see her again.

"Stasis engaged."

The universe went black.

TWO

Anna had scarcely set foot in the Sclerophyll Biome before she came face to face with Darth Vader. "Only you could be so bold," she said, shaking her head. "If the Senate only knew that you're the best dad in the galaxy, they'd hurry up and terraform Elysium, so you could head down there and show them your skills. Now, out of my way – the new eggs are hatching, and I need to be there. No amount of fluffing about by you is going to stop me." She pushed past the agitated emu and marched toward the shed.

She had a video feed set up, ready to capture the first ever images of a Baudin's dwarf emu chick, which would also be the first of its kind seen in almost a thousand years, since they'd been driven extinct by short-sighted colonists back on Earth. This Colony would bring them back to life and hopefully give them a fighting chance to survive well into the future.

Well, if they survived into adulthood here, like Darth and his brood.

She palmed open the door, letting it

hiss shut behind her before activating the inner door. Not quite an airlock, but it did help to keep the temperature constant inside when outside could vary a bit. And it kept the emus from mixing before they were supposed to.

Only one incubator sat in the cavern-like space, where she could easily fit a dozen, if she needed to. Not this time, though – this one precious clutch of eggs occupied all her attention. If she could raise even one of these babies to adulthood, then she had a chance to bring back all the extinct emu species. Maybe even moa.

But first, these babies had to hatch.

Anna sank down onto the floor beside the incubator. The first cracks had appeared about an hour ago, when she was finishing up her lunch, but she'd known she had at least an hour or two before the first baby emerged, and a couple hours more before the chicks would be out of the eggs entirely. She'd promised Prometheus the footage, so he could do a time lapse with a feature on the dwarf emus, if they survived. Even if they didn't these tiny babies would be famous. Poor Darth would be so jealous if he knew.

But wait…was that movement? One egg was rocking, a piece of the shell lifting away just the littlest bit…

Every second she watched felt like forever, and yet it was over quite quickly. The chick just kept butting its little head against that shell, pushing the pieces higher a little each time, until the egg toppled over on its side, cracking in half from the force of the fall.

The chick, sensing victory, pushed again, until the two halves split apart and the baby bird sprawled on the warm floor of the incubator.

Anna peered at it, watching to see if it was still breathing. Thankfully, it was. Carefully, she reached into the incubator to take out the bits of broken shell. She'd done it. The first Baudin's dwarf emu to be born into the Altan system, right here. She could be more proud than if she'd given birth herself. More, maybe, seeing as giving birth to a human baby only required a bit of sex, followed by nine months of carrying it around in your belly, which any fertile human could accomplish, while bringing an extinct bird back to life for the first time would have earned her all sorts of accolades from her colleagues back on Earth, Mars and the other planets of the Solar system. A pity they'd never know.

If only Valentine were here to see it. He'd understand. He'd been there on Titan when she'd first started this quest, and he'd seen so many failures along the way. That he hadn't lived long enough to see the first real success…it was that stupid war that had killed him. He'd joined the fight to protect her, he'd said, as an engineer and not a fighter, but the fighting had taken him anyway, when the *Magellan*, the ship he'd served on, had been blown up in a battle.

That had been four years ago. Four long, lonely years, wishing he'd never joined the war effort, watching the war end in a truce so anticlimactic, even she wasn't sure what they'd been fighting for. Had Valentine died for nothing?

In the darkest hours of the night, it wasn't the why of Valentine's death that worried her, but the when and how. She hoped it had been quick and painless, but no one had been able to tell her. They'd called off the search for survivors after three months. Soon after that was when she'd finally lost hope that she'd ever seen him again.

Her tablet chimed – an incoming message from the hospital. Strange – she wasn't sick or injured. Perhaps they wanted her for a routine checkup? Ah, that must be it. She swiped to open the message, only to discover it was a live video call.

"Dr Anna Gulis?" the woman on the screen asked.

"Yes, that's me," Anna said.

"Dr Gulis, it's about your husband."

Anna almost dropped her tablet in surprise. "I'll be right there."

THREE

"I'm here to see Valentine Gulis, please," Anna said breathlessly to the hospital receptionist.

The woman blinked at her, then lowered her eyes to her tablet. "Friend or relative?"

"I'm his wi…wife," Anna said. Stars, she'd almost said she was his widow.

Well, until she'd received that message, she'd thought she was a widow. Now…she could barely believe it.

The receptionist nodded. "He's in Regen, on Level Four. Take the blue elevator, then follow the signs to Regeneration."

Regeneration? She'd heard about it, of course, as a treatment offered by a few, very exclusive clinics on Earth. Clinics that you could only use if your parents had chosen to preserve your stem cells at birth, for an exorbitant sum, of course, which was barely a pittance compared to the cost of taking those cells out of stasis to regenerate parts of your body that you'd lost or needed replacing.

Definitely not something her family or Valentine's could afford, or either of them now they were adults. Besides, even if Valentine's family had preserved his stem cells, there's no way they would've been aboard the *Genesis*.

So she'd go to Regen, find out where Valentine really was, and go there next.

But at the front desk in Regen, the receptionist didn't even pause to look at her tablet. "Ward Five," she said, pointing.

Anna took a deep breath before stepping inside Ward Five. It didn't look like any hospital ward she'd ever seen before. More like an aquarium, with a row of cylindrical glass tanks that bubbled softly.

The only light in the room came from the tablets clipped to each tank, each bearing a different name. GULIS,

Valentine was on the end.

Anna cupped her hands around her eyes and peered into Valentine's tank. She could faintly see a shadowy form that might be human, but there was no way of telling if it was Valentine.

Somehow, she found herself back at Regen reception. "Um, I'm not sure…this isn't what I expected…are you sure Valentine Gulis is here?" she asked.

The receptionist looked her up and down. "You're not a doctor, then?"

Anna smiled faintly. "Well, I am, but not a medical doctor. My PhD's in ornithology. I work in Eden Labs, raising birds for terraforming. I was with the emus when I got the call, telling me Valentine is…was…is…he's my husband. When I heard, I came straight here."

Sympathy dawned on the receptionist's face. "Oh, I see. Whoever called you should have been more clear, then. We've been notifying the families as patients' identities become known, but Valentine Gulis took some time to identify because his pod was damaged. We don't get many visitors for the patients in Regen. Not until they're released to the normal wards on Level Three."

"But I'm here…and…if he's really here…I thought he was dead. Are you sure it's him? How can you tell?" Anna asked.

The receptionist shrugged. "Some of them had identification on their uniforms when they went into stasis. The rest of have been identified by surviving members of the *Magellan* crew. Valentine…he needed more regeneration than the others, because of the damage to the pod, before any kind of facial recognition was possible."

"Oh stars…" Tears poured out of Anna's eyes, too fast for her to stop. "How badly was he hurt?"

The receptionist shook her head. "I'm sorry, Mrs Gulis, but we won't know for sure until he's well enough to leave the tank and wake up. We can regenerate most of the human body now, but even if brain cells grow back, we can't replace the memories that were lost. So while we can be sure your husband's healthy body is in that tank, the man who wakes up in it might not be the husband you knew."

"Is there…is there anything I can do?" Anna asked, even as she knew there was nothing.

The receptionist shrugged. "Talk to him, if you like. Ward Five is for final stage regeneration. Their vital stats have to be within normal ranges or an alarm sounds, so they have normal heartbeat, brain activity, everything. He can probably hear you, inside the tank. Just like a coma patient, really. Talk to him. The patients here don't get many visitors, so it's up to you. If you want to go home and wait for someone to call you when he's released to a ward downstairs…"

Anna took a deep breath. "No, I'll talk to him. I never thought I'd get the chance to talk to him again. So…I will."

She forced her feet to carry her back to Ward Five, and the tank where Valentine's ghostly form hung suspended in the water.

She'd lost count of the number of times she'd wished she could talk to her husband one more time. Now she had her wish…and she didn't know what to say.

FOUR

The first sound he heard was a woman clearing her throat. Nervous, yet muffled – like she was covering her mouth with her hand. Or on the other side of a door.

"I…they said I should talk to you. That it might help you wake up. If you're going to wake up. They couldn't even tell me that…"

A muffled sob, then another.

His heart went out to her, this poor woman and whoever she was talking to. Some poor bastard in worse shape than him, if the doctors didn't even know if he'd live or die.

"When I…when I first heard the news about the *Magellan*, and every day since, I keep replaying the same conversation we had on the day we met, and how I didn't really tell you the truth. Well, I didn't lie, but I didn't tell you everything, either. I've wanted to tell you for so long, but it never seemed the right time. Partly because it wasn't just my story to tell, but also because…I guess I was scared of what you might say. What you'd think of me. But I think you should know, so I'm going to tell you, even if you can't hear me. Even if I have to tell you again sometime, if you wake up. Because…the second time will be easier. At least, that's what the grief counsellors say. Maybe it's just a tactic to get you to talk when you don't want to. Maybe there won't ever be a second time, because you're not going to make it and the doctors already know but they're not going to tell me yet because they don't know if I can take it. Or maybe it's not even you in there, and they've made a mistake, mixed you up with someone else, and you died out there in space, just like they told me…"

Silence. It stretched and stretched, until he wondered if she'd left, her footsteps so quiet he'd never heard them.

Poor woman. He wanted to offer his sympathies, for the loss of whoever she was talking to, but it sounded like spilling her deepest secrets was something she wanted to do, before she gave in to the grief for her loss.

"You asked me why I wasn't afraid. And I told you it was because of my favourite book when I was a kid. Knowing my parents, they probably still have it, stuffed into a bookcase somewhere, ready to show you when we came to visit, before telling you the whole story, but then the bombs went off and we had to board the *Genesis* and there was no time…so we never did get to visit. And then the attack on the lab and the war and…now if I don't tell you, I might never. So it started with a book, a bottle of water, and a mushy cheese sandwich, all bundled up into a backpack that was the last thing my mother ever gave me, before she abandoned me at the zoo.

"I remember seeing my first real emu, so excited I squealed out loud. I remember sitting on a rock to eat a cheese sandwich, high up so I could see the emu browsing through the bushes on the other side of the enclosure. I remember taking my book out of my bag, turning the pages to compare the real, live emu with the one in the pictures, until I heard a strange noise, and found myself face to face with the emu. It was a free range enclosure, you see, where you could walk through with them. This one liked to sit on the rock I'd perched on, so when it came and sat beside me, I just shuffled over and started showing it my book.

"When the zoo closed, or maybe the next morning when it opened, I don't remember, one of the keepers found me, asleep with my head on the emu's back. I cried when they shooed the emu away, and as they took me to the office and then the police station before I inevitably ended up in the hands of Child Protection. They sent me to a bunch of foster homes, one after the other, but all I wanted was to go back to the zoo, and I told them so. So one of the foster carers took pity on me and did take me to the zoo.

"I was so excited. I couldn't stop talking about how I wanted to see him again, but everywhere we went, there weren't any emus. Somehow, the idea took hold in my head that when they'd shooed him away, he'd gone for good, and he wasn't there any more. I was so upset, but the carer just wouldn't listen. I will never forget the sight of her, spit flying from her mouth, as she screamed at me that my daddy wasn't here, he'd never be here again, because he didn't want me, and if I didn't shut up about him, no one else would want me, either.

"Child Protection sent me to another foster home after that. And I cried there, too, until they took me to the zoo.

"Except this time was different. You see, Child Protection have their bigots and their favourites, and the case worker who'd been assigned to me was a bigot of the worst kind…and I definitely wasn't her favourite. So she sent me as the very first foster child to a gay couple, without much background at all. She wanted them to fail, and she wanted me to be the tool she used to make it happen.

"Of course, Rick and Marco, both lawyers, were too smart to let some petty bigot take away their chance at parenthood. So they did the one thing none of the others had – while we were waiting in line to get in, Rick asked me which animal was my favourite, the one I wanted to see most. And when we got in, they took me straight to the emu enclosure, where I climbed up on that rock, happy to have finally found my emu, or at least the bird I thought was my emu. I couldn't tell them apart then. And my new foster carers…they sat next to me on that same rock, and just watched the emus.

"When it was time for the zoo to close, Rick asked me why I loved emus so much. And I told him about my favourite book, which I'd insisted my mother read to me over and over, about a daddy emu who took care of his baby, and because I had no daddy, I wanted a daddy emu to take care of me, too.

"I don't actually remember this part, but Rick and Marco have told the story so many times, I know the words by heart. They sat with me on that rock, with the emu looking on, and they told me that the daddy emu was only taking care of me until they found me, and now they were both going to be my daddies, because I was so precious I needed two of them, and they'd take care of me as long as I needed them to, until I was all grown up. Marco swears the emu nodded like he agreed with them, and then they took me home.

"They were my parents, my family, from then on. Sure, we went to the zoo a lot, and there were other foster kids, some who stayed, too, but I never forgot that emu, who sat with me when I was afraid. So I can never be afraid of emus. And when the opportunity arose to repay the favour, to bring back some emu species that had gone extinct, and raise more emus to increase the number of good dads in the galaxy…well, I guess I couldn't resist. And my two dads encouraged me to follow that dream, so here I am. Here we are. And I'm…oh,

I'm so sorry you got hurt for it. If I'd known I'd lose you, that war would break out here…I never would have…I would have…

The words ended in sobbing, followed by running footsteps.

Now she was gone.

He sighed. Poor woman. She'd lost everything, and now she was losing the last family she had left. Somehow, he doubted a bird would step in to help her now.

FIVE

"How was your Valentine's Day?"

Anna jumped. She hadn't told anyone about Valentine. How…who…

Lilith held up her hands in a gesture of surrender. "Sorry, I didn't mean to scare you. I thought you heard me come in. I guess that means you didn't get much sleep last night. So, who was your hot Valentine's date?"

Anna willed her heart to stop hammering. Lilith didn't know about her husband, she'd been talking about Valentine's Day. Valentine's birthday, and she hadn't even remembered. What did you buy a man who spent his days swimming in a tank? Flippers? Anna smothered a laugh.

"Come on, it's not like Rocail would ever remember something as romantic as Valentine's Day, so I have to live vicariously through single girls like you. Tell me everything," Lilith said, lifting her coffee cup to her lips.

Anna ducked her head to break the stare from Lilith's eager eyes. "I'm not single. I still feel like I'm married to a ghost. I spent last night in bed, alone, wishing he was there with me. There's nothing to tell, unless you want to know how many tissues it took to mop up my tears. Ask Eve or Vega if you want to hear about dating adventures. Dating isn't in my future, or at least the future I can see."

Lilith's eyes widened. "You mean you didn't have a hot date with Orel last night? Stars, I could've sworn that rose was for you. I wonder who the lucky girl is?"

"Orel?" Anna considered the shy cupid. He was a lovely boy, really, always willing to help. She hadn't heard that he was dating anyone, but then Orel wasn't one to say much. She hoped whoever he'd spent last night with was someone as sweet as he was. "You'd have to ask him, I think."

"Like he'll tell me. He runs at the sight of me, now. That's Rocail's fault, always making me chase him up over Rocail's requests." Lilith shook her head. "Sometimes, I wonder what I see in him."

Orel? What she saw in Orel? It took Anna's fuddled brain a moment to realise she'd been talking about Rocail. Anna didn't know the man very well, seeing as they worked in different parts of Eden, but what she did know… "Well, he's very driven. Brilliant, successful. Passionate about his work…" And a ruthless arsehole who'd experiment on his own mother if he thought it would further his career. She'd heard rumours…

"And don't forget, he knows his way around the female anatomy better than any sculptor. When he's willing to put in the effort…" Lilith's face scrunched up. "I can't remember the last time he gave me an orgasm. Lately, it's all about him…"

Anna nodded, letting Lilith's complaints wash over her without actually hearing them. Valentine had always been amazing in the bedroom, or any room, really, planetside or space. The things he could do in zero g…

"What do you think?" Lilith asked suddenly.

Anna blinked. Slowly, she said, "I think that it's your life, and you deserve to be happy with someone who loves and values you as you deserve. And if that's Rocail or someone else entirely…that's a decision only you can make. And no one is more qualified to make it than you."

Lilith managed a watery smile. "Thanks, Anna. I…don't think I'm ready to make a decision, one way or the other, right now, but I should probably sleep on it. Alone, as usual."

Being alone was miserable, as Anna well knew. "You should take some of these strawberries with you. Something sweet always helps."

"Are you sure you don't want them?"

Anna shook her head. "I took home a big chunk of watermelon yesterday. At this rate, I'll be having it for breakfast, lunch and dinner until it's gone. Even after all this time, I forget I don't have anyone at home to share it with." Maybe she should take her dinner into the hospital, and sit beside Valentine's tank while she ate. Better than being alone.

"Thanks, Anna. Strawberries aren't as good as hot sex, but maybe I could borrow one of those hot romances from the library to read while I eat…"

"Sounds like a plan," Anna said. Lilith could read about her imaginary hero, while Anna could sit beside Valentine again.

Never mind that he was stuck in a tank. One day, he'd be well enough to leave hospital, and she'd have her husband back.

Now that would be something to celebrate.

SIX

"Do you remember the fruit baskets we had on our honeymoon? I remember laughing at you when you wanted that cruise ship because of the fruit, but by the time we reached Saturn, I was craving an apple so badly, I nearly knocked you over to get to the basket."

The bird woman was back to visit her

husband.

He wasn't sure if he'd woken up in the middle of her visit, or whether she'd just arrived and started to speak. She had the sweetest voice, and she used it well to tell a bloody good story, too. He was willing to bet she read bedtime stories to her kids every night in that voice, or she would, if she and her husband didn't have them yet.

"I try not to remember it, seeing as it wasn't my finest moment, but you never forgot, and never let me forget, either, any time we bought apples. We don't have apples here in the Colony yet – the trees aren't old enough to produce fruit yet, even with enhanced growth rates. Sometimes I forget how far out in space we are and I think I'm still in the labs on

Titan, trialling those new artificial eggshells for penguins and moa.

"Especially yesterday. I spent all day revising the protocols for moa embryos, because now the Baudin's emus are doing okay, it's time to start on the moa. I went into the lunchroom to get a coffee, and Orel was there with a couple of ripe watermelons from the Alvarium Biome. He cut one open, and just that sweet smell was enough to send me back to Titan, and all those times the moa didn't make it. I'd cry my eyes out, and you'd go down to the hydroponics level, work your magic, and come back with a watermelon to cheer me up.

"I don't know how much melon I ate yesterday, but by the end of the day, I'd almost completely rewritten the protocols. We've tested them so many times on emus, that I'm sure it's the thickness. Coupled with the conditions in the incubator, and…you'll have to come see the babies when they're born. They will survive this time. I'm certain of it.

"Anyway, Orel gave me the rest of the watermelon to take home, as if I needed any more of it, and I was too polite to refuse. Then again, after all the ration bars I've been eating lately, fresh fruit is such a treat. I hope you don't mind that I brought my dinner here. I'll try not to drip any juice on the floor, or clean it up if I do. Stars know what the nurses will do if I don't. They might not let me come visit you again."

A long pause, before he found he

could hear the sound of soft crunching.

Watermelon. The bird woman was eating watermelon here.

His mouth watered. He could almost feel the way the watermelon crushed between his teeth, sweetness exploding on his tongue. He couldn't remember the last time he'd tasted watermelon, it had been so long.

How long?

It must be…

He couldn't remember the last time.

He tried, and…nothing.

Like someone had gone through his head and wiped his memories clean. But why watermelon?

Why wipe just his memories of watermelon?

What else had he forgotten?

He racked his brain, trying to remember the last thing he'd eaten. Or the last thing he remembered eating. Anything. Any memory at all.

Stars, where were they? Why couldn't he remember anything?

"Dr Gulis, is everything all right?" This voice was new.

"I think he's in pain, he's thrashing about terribly. Is there anything you can give him to help him?"

"We've been trying to reduce the medication, in preparation for taking him out of the tank. Perhaps a light sedative will help…"

While their attention was fixed on the bird woman's husband, he tried to calm his whirling thoughts. Whirling like a black hole, no memories or light escaping…why couldn't he remember?

Black hole sucking him in…he surrendered, as he knew he must.

He only hoped there'd be fresh watermelon on the other side.

SEVEN

"Dr Gulis, you should go home. He'll be out for hours, so there's no reason to stay." Dr Calmana said.

Anna wrung her hands. "Are you sure? But he's in pain, you said. What if…what if it's because of the stem cells used in the treatment?" Stars only knew where the cells had come from, because they couldn't possibly have been Valentine's.

Anna recognised the professional smile spreading across the other woman's face. It was the smile you wore when dealing with someone who knew nothing about your area of expertise.

"Dr Gulis, I assure you, your husband's stem cells were in a perfect state of preservation, and his regeneration has proceeded exactly as we would expect, with such excellent material to work with. Better, even. I only wish the stem cell banks on the *Titanic* had been as robust as the ones on the *Genesis*. As it is, your husband is on schedule for a complete recovery, something we can only thank the state of the art facilities in the Colony for."

Anna swallowed. "But you don't

understand. Valentine didn't have any stem cells preserved on the *Genesis*. Whatever cells you used, they can't have been his."

Calmana frowned. "That can't be right. They were an exact DNA match. Unless your husband has an identical twin…"

Anna shook her head. "Valentine was an only child. He didn't have any brothers."

The doctor held up her hands. "Look, I don't know about the provenance of the stem cells before I received them, but I do know they were an exact genetic match to his own cells, as evident by his recovery."

"But you said he was in pain…" Anna's heart squeezed in her chest at the thought of Valentine hurting.

"That's a normal part of the growth process, as existing tissue knits with new growth. Pain is a good sign — it means his nervous system, all the way up to his brain, is working well. In fact, it's usually a pretty good indicator that he'll be ready to leave the tank soon."

Anna found herself nodding. Where the cells had come from was a mystery for another time. What mattered was that they'd worked, and, against all odds, she'd be getting Valentine back.

"I'll see that one of my staff calls you when he's ready for visitors," Dr Calmana said.

EIGHT

Balmy warmth embraced him, while something scratchy rustled at his back. When footsteps came, they sounded clearer. Closer. Instead of like he was at the bottom of a well, while the rest of the world went on above.

Actually, the warmth was getting to be a bit much. He felt uncomfortably hot all over, like he'd spent too much time in the sun. He had a sudden flash of running around naked in the desert, before it was gone, but the burning sensation on his skin remained. He'd felt like this then.

"What in the stars were you thinking?" a female voice shrieked, before a clatter of metal as something rolled rapidly across the floor drowned out any reply. The sound stopped as she said, "I don't care what standard procedure is for giving patients vitamin D – Regen patients get supplements only, not a bloody sunlamp! Do you know how delicate that skin is? Like a newborn's, you idiot, and now he's red as a lobster! You'd better hope he doesn't need to go back in the tank for this. You have no idea…"

Her voice faded along with her footsteps.

He must have drifted off, because the next thing he knew, someone was rubbing what felt like sandpaper across his skin. He tried to tell them to go away, politely at first, and then more colourfully, but it didn't matter. The words just wouldn't come out, like there was something wrong with his throat, or his mouth.

"It's all right. This is the new burn enzyme. It'll heal you right up, like you'd never been in the sun, I promise. I know it feels a bit rough going on, but there's a numbing agent in it that'll start working right away. It was invented right here in the Colony, and while I admit it's still experimental – one or two short-term side effects that last for a week or so afterwards – it does the job beautifully. Even Dr Calmana won't be able to complain." The nurse let out a little laugh. "Okay, she probably will complain about something – she's very protective of her patients, and given how much you've had to regrow, I guess I understand, but…" The words washed over him, and he stopped listening.

Hospital gossip meant nothing to him.

Blessed numbness started to spread across his skin, and he drifted away again.

NINE

He couldn't remember the last time he'd eaten, but surely it had to be better than the ration pack nutrient soup in his bowl right now. They'd given him a spoon to eat it with, but he knew the best thing to do with this goop was to drink it down as quickly as possible, because the less he tasted, the better.

He'd slurped a little too slowly and the taste hit his tongue. Like a combination of meat and cabbage and week-old bread, with a strong aftertaste of chemical-laced cardboard. He wanted to throw it up again, but the taste of it coming back up again would be worse. Not to mention he'd already been assured that if he wasn't feeling well enough to eat yet, he could be fed intravenously, as if that was supposed to be reassuring.

No, he was a grown man who wanted out of this hospital room, so he gritted his teeth before taking another big gulp. He'd had this foul-tasting stuff before, must have, if he'd known how bad it was, but he couldn't summon a single memory about it. Either he'd tried to block it out, or the memory was just gone. He wasn't sure which was worse.

Finally, he set the empty soup bowl down and reached for his cup of water. That tasted fine, and he used some of it to swish the remains of the soup from his mouth before swallowing the lot. He reached for the jug to pour another cup.

And stopped halfway there, because he'd know those footsteps anywhere — they belonged to the bird woman.

His eyes darted to the door as he prayed he'd see her, if only for a moment, as she went past.

The universe answered his prayer as her footsteps slowed, then stopped...right in the doorway.

His heart stopped. She was the loveliest woman he'd ever seen. It almost hurt to look at her, knowing she was here to see her husband and not him.

He forced his fingers to close around the handle of the jug, keeping his eyes on the water level in his cup so they wouldn't return to her.

He felt her gaze on him, though. The horror in her eyes as she looked at him. He hadn't summoned the courage to ask for a mirror yet, to see the scars for himself that made him into a monster she couldn't bear to look at.

"Wrong room, lady. Go back to reception or the nurses station, and they'll tell you where to find your husband," he said gruffly.

She opened her mouth like she wanted to say something. Thank you, maybe, or ask how he'd gotten so scarred. Then she pressed her lips together, nodded mutely, and bolted.

He closed his eyes. He should never have looked at her. Now he knew for certain that her husband was the luckiest bastard in the world, and he himself sat firmly at the opposite end of the spectrum where it came to luck.

Why had anyone bothered to regenerate him, if all his future held was frightened looks from people who considered him a monster? They should've just let him die.

TEN

"Dr Gulis, wait!"

Anna forced her feet to stop, though she just wanted to keep running. Valentine hadn't recognised her. Hadn't known who she was. She wanted to run right back to the last night they'd spent together, just after the war broke out, and beg him not to go. To lose him now, when she'd thought she'd have him back…it hurt too much to bear.

"What's wrong?" Dr Calmana asked. "Couldn't you find his room? I'll take you, if you like. I was just about to tell him the results from his last round of tests."

Anna shook her head. "I found the room fine. But the man in it…isn't my husband. My husband would never dismiss me like that. Wouldn't tell me I had the wrong room. Wouldn't turn his face away instead of greeting me, telling me how much he'd missed me. Without some sign that he at least recognised me. That man…I don't know him, and he definitely doesn't know me." She hurried out before Valentine's doctor could stop her again.

As she sped toward the aircar station, she considered stopping at the Chocolaterie for a box of chocolates. No, it would cost her half a year's salary, maybe more, for enough chocolate to make her feel better today. And she wouldn't be able to afford food, let alone more chocolate, tomorrow. Better to drown her sorrows in drink at one of the many pubs in Metropolis City.

Not that she drank often, but when she did, she favoured the fizz they served at Forge. Maybe if she told them she'd lost her husband for the second time, they'd sell her a bottle she could take home. No way did she want to get blind drunk in a bar with other people. Better to be at home alone, where she was less likely to embarrass herself.

But even as she crossed the square, she couldn't bring herself to go into the pub. She'd been a widow for a while now, and not once had she given in. No, instead of alcohol, she'd drowned herself in work, because that's what Valentine would have wanted. She was here in space to save the emus and every other extinct species that could have a future here. It was his legacy, and it would be hers when she was gone.

Her birds needed her alert, not drinking her way to the bottom of a bottle.

Anna nodded to herself as she boarded the aircar to Eden. Yes. Work would save her from grief. It had gotten her this far, and she was needed there.

Even if Valentine would never need

her again.

Anna sucked back a sob, hoping no one else in the aircar had noticed.

She'd spent so long bringing species back from the dead, that she'd never stopped to think whether it was right to do the same to people. Now she knew the answer, it was cold comfort for a grieving widow.

Anna straightened. She might be a grieving widow, but she was also a mother of sorts, to the baby Baudin's emus, and she'd be the only mother the first generation moa knew.

She clapped her hands together. Yes, that's what she'd do — implant the first set of moa embryos into their eggs tonight.

ELEVEN

Dr Calmana entered the room, and Valentine lifted his head to meet her eyes. "What's up, Doc?" he asked.

"Before I tell you about your test results, I want to ask you about what you remember," she said.

He shrugged. "Hearing you shout at the orderly who gave me too much vitamin D."

Her eyes narrowed, as if this was news to her. Maybe she hadn't expected him to remember that. "No, I mean before that. Anything about the accident that brought you here into hospital?"

Running naked through the desert. He couldn't even remember why he'd done it. But he did know he hadn't ended up in hospital for that. That'd been years ago, another life. Not here. Though he didn't even know where here was.

"Nope. Not a thing. Pity, because I'm sure I've eaten better food than this hospital serves. I just wish I could remember it."

Something flickered, out of the corner of his eye. Movement, up near the ceiling. He stared upwards, waiting for it to happen again.

He barely caught it — a flicker of the lights, as they brightened, then dimmed.

"That's not a good sign. Fluctuations in the power like that mean your power plant's at risk of overheating, or worse, overloading. Someone should check that out before it's too late to fix." He found the doctor staring at him. "What? Don't ask me how I know that, but I just do. Fusion power's weakness is its coolant system. Everyone knows that."

The doctor waited, as if expecting him to say more, but he was done. Eventually, she sighed, then said, "Keep trying. It should come back to you."

He folded his arms across his chest. "Not going to give me a hint, Doc? Something that might jog my memory, maybe?"

She spread her arms wide and shrugged. "I would if I could, but I wasn't there. A salvage crew found you in a badly damaged escape pod in the asteroid field, before bringing you here. We weren't sure if we could save you, and it was touch and go for the first few weeks, but then you started to respond to the stem cell treatments, and now here we are."

"But where's here, Doc?"

"The hospital, of course, in Metropolis City."

"Never heard of it."

She blinked. "Oh, of course. The Colony wasn't built when the *Magellan* went down. Metropolis City is the centre of a multi-dome settlement on New

Hope, the seventh planet in the Altan system."

None of the names rang a bell, except for Altan. Something about forty light years away from Earth. Far from home, now it was home. He searched his feelings, looking for something, anything, to tell him about his past. But there was nothing…just that vague feeling of rightness, that Altan was home.

"Home sweet Hope, or New Hope, anyway," he said.

She inclined her head. "That will be up to you to decide, when you're well enough to leave, of course. Best to focus on your recovery, and let the future worry about itself." She pulled out a tablet and began scrolling through what he could only assume were his blood test results.

He knew he should listen to her, but he couldn't shake the thought of how a man who couldn't remember his past could possibly have a future, here or anywhere.

TWELVE

At first, she'd meant to only prepare enough eggs for one incubator, but then she'd started preparing the embryos for implantation in the eggs, and somehow she'd forgotten she was dealing with moa and not emus, and she was staring at a double batch of embryos, about to start on a third. Anna even had the next vial in her hand, and she couldn't remember taking the rack out of stasis. She squinted at the label, brushing condensation off it so she could read it clearly. Aquila? No, it should say Pachyornis! Quickly, she checked a couple of other vials in the same rack — all Aquila — before putting the rack back into stasis. There was a place for eagles in the Altan system, but it wasn't her moa biome. Not yet.

What if she'd…

Anna fished out one of the empty vials from the racks she'd already implanted. No, that said Pachyornis, like it was supposed to. Thank the stars she'd stopped when she did.

She carefully loaded the eggs into the incubators, the programmed in the new protocol. This time it would be different

— surely some of the embryos would survive, unlike all the embryos she'd lost on Titan. She couldn't wait to see what a baby moa looked like.

Once she'd sealed both incubators, she picked up her tablet to make a note of the settings, as well as the date and time. She'd need to monitor these more carefully than the emus, so that if something went wrong, she'd know precisely where, in order to improve on the process next time.

The door to the lab whooshed open. "You're in early," Vega said, still buttoning her lab coat over her green coverall. "Or are you working late?"

Anna glanced at the menu bar on her tablet, which told her it was 7:32 already. She'd worked all night? She hadn't pulled an all nighter since the week she'd received the news about the *Magellan*'s demise. Maybe a couple weeks after that, too — she had to admit those first few weeks had become a blur in her mind. Much like last night.

The tablet in her hands pinged, as if in rebuke, and she almost dropped it in surprise. No, it wasn't suddenly sentient. It was just pinging to alert her to an incoming message. A text message, thank the stars, from Dr Calmana. Brief but to the point:

Your husband is suffering from amnesia. Unsure yet whether this is temporary or how much of it is permanent. Would like to meet at the hospital so we can discuss possible paths forward for his treatment.

A small, cowardly part of Anna didn't want to meet the doctor at all, but she knew she couldn't avoid the woman forever. Couldn't avoid the man who had been her husband, either. The sooner she faced up to this, the sooner she could move on with her life. If that was even possible…

"Can you keep an eye on these? Hourly observations. I need to go up to the hops…the hops…" Stars take it, she couldn't even get the word out right.

Vega shook her head. "I'll monitor the new eggs in the incubator, but only if you go home and get some sleep. Everything else can wait."

It could, couldn't it? She didn't have to face Valentine and Dr Calmana now. She could…sleep…and see them later.

Anna tapped out a brief message, telling the doctor she'd visit the hospital this evening. Putting it off, but still committing to action, if a little delayed. Maybe she wasn't as much of a coward as she thought.

Anna staggered out of the lab, and up to her apartment. The door had scarcely slid closed behind her before she fell, face first, onto the bed and sleep claimed her for its own.

THIRTEEN

He glided into her slick heat, savouring the taste of her on his tongue. A fine sheen of sweat glimmered on her skin as her breasts bobbed in the low gravity, a counterpoint to the rhythm of her rocking hips. So beautiful. The most perfect woman he'd ever met, touched…

She regarded him through half-lidded

eyes, as blissed out from their lovemaking as he was. How long had they been doing this? Half the night, at least, but he never wanted to stop. He needed her like he needed air, and when they were together…taking her to the very pinnacle of pleasure was as instinctive as breathing.

As if on cue, her breathing quickened, and then she began to moan. He felt her tightening around him, her timing so perfect it seemed even the universe wanted them to be together in everything.

"Oh yes, oh yes, oh YES…" she breathed, slowing her movements even as he did.

Her cries soared over his triumphant bellow as twin orgasms enveloped them both.

As he regained his vision, he found her lips sliding up his length.

"We can't. I can't," he groaned as she sucked on him. She had a husband, loved someone else, couldn't possibly be in bed with him…

He sat up with a start. Blank hospital walls stared back at him, condemning him for lusting after another man's wife. Stars help him, he had the mother of all hard-ons, and a hospital was hardly the place to be caught doing anything about it, what with nurses and orderlies wandering in and out.

What if the bird woman walked in and saw him like this? Dreaming about her was one thing, but to see her in the flesh, after fantasising about her naked…stars, he wasn't sure he could look her in the eye after that. Not that she'd come into his hospital room again — she'd made that mistake once, and wouldn't make it again. Hopefully, she'd found her husband and now he'd only see and hear her in his dreams.

Searingly hot, erotic dreams. Stars…

He started to drift off to sleep again, but she was waiting for him, wearing nothing more than an eager smile. And he was helpless to resist…

FOURTEEN

Dr Calmana didn't even wait for Anna to sit down before she began. "When we first contacted you about your husband, we told you there could be some lasting effects from his injuries. It's worst case scenario, but it's always best to warn the patient's family, especially when there's brain damage. Physically, Mr Gulis has made a remarkable recovery when those first few weeks, when we weren't even sure he would survive. However, temporary or even permanent amnesia is likely where parts of the brain required regeneration. We can regrow the cells, but it's up to the patient to remap those internal networks, with their own thoughts and memories. New ones to replace the old ones that were lost.

"Mr Gulis does have flashes of memory, but they're returning slowly. There are no certainties when it comes to the Human brain, or its memories. He might come to remember everything about your time together, or none of it. He will have some permanent memory loss, but the rest should come back."

Anna folded her arms across her chest.

"So you're saying I should just be patient, and I'll get my husband back eventually? Or at least part of him? In…what? A year? Two? Ten? And I'm supposed to care for him like an invalid until he remembers who he is?"

Calmana ducked her head, almost as if she was hiding a smile. Yet when she raised her eyes to meet Anna's again, she was all seriousness. "Actually, Mr Gulis is in almost perfect physical health. If it wasn't procedure to keep regen patients under observation for at least seven days out of the tank, I could release him into your care right now, and he would be as physically capable as any other person in the Colony. Well, any adult, anyway. There's no question about whether he can function as a capable member of the

Colony." She leaned forward. "The question is how active a part you'd like to play in his recovery."

Anna stared at her. "You're not asking whether I'm willing to help him use the toilet. What are you asking?"

Calmana wet her lips. "Well, under Altan Senate law, an Altan citizen can be declared dead after they've been involved in a disaster and no sign of life has been found for a year after the disaster. The *Magellan* was lost well over a year ago, so you're well within your rights to declare that death has dissolved your marriage and that Valentine Gulis is no longer your husband. As his wife, you're his next of kin, but as his ex-wife, you'd have no responsibility for him whatsoever. In fact, you'd be well within your rights to never have contact with him again, if that was your wish."

NO. The word sounded so loud in Anna's head she almost thought she'd shouted it, but her lips remained closed. Lose Valentine again, for the third and final time? She couldn't even consider it. If there was any chance he was anywhere near the man she'd known and married, she couldn't desert him. In sickness and in health, for death had not actually parted them yet.

"Will he recover any of his memories?" Anna asked.

The doctor spread her hands wide. "I can't be certain. The memories he's lost may have shaped him as a person, which means that the person he becomes now might be radically different from the man you knew. He has the same DNA, but he might be as similar to Mr Gulis as his twin, or a clone. Not the same man at all. I am confident that he will regain some of his memories, but I have no idea which ones. If you were to wash your hands of him now, and tell me that, under the disaster death laws, he is no longer your husband, I am certain he could live an active and fulfilling life in the career of his choice, without you. He might never remember you, or the life you have together." She pressed her lips together, as if unwilling to give voice to the other thought that followed her statement.

Anna had no such qualms. "Or he could remember everything, and spend the rest of his life wondering about, maybe even mourning, the wife who left him when he was at his weakest."

Dr Calmana held up her hands. "There's no guarantee that he will remember, but even if he did, there's nothing to stop either of you from reconnecting."

Anna laughed. "Oh, I think there would be. I wouldn't want to reconnect with some callous, uncaring bitch who walked away from me if I was in hospital, and nor would Valentine. Do you have a spouse, Dr Calmana?" Anna would bet every credit she earned in a year that Calmana was single.

The doctor bowed her head. "No. No, I haven't been lucky enough to find the right person, someone I'd want to spend the rest of my life with."

"Then you have no idea what we would and wouldn't do for each other. If the man in that hospital room is my husband, if any shred of him remains, then only death itself could tear us apart. No, not even death, seeing as you've brought him back from the brink for me. He wouldn't give up on me. Not if there was even the slightest hope. And I won't give up on him!"

"But he may never remember you, or the time you spent together. Those memories might have been in the damaged brain cells we had to regrow."

"Then we'll make new memories. Better than the first ones."

Anna rose from her seat and stormed out of the doctor's office, nearly bowling into a woman who stood outside. She mumbled an apology, then made a beeline for Valentine.

FIFTEEN

She was back. He'd know those footsteps anywhere, waking or sleeping. The bird woman was back. He sat up in bed, craning his neck as he hoped for a glimpse of her as she went past. He might have spent all night dreaming about her, but he needed to see her again to familiarise himself with the lines of her face, the way she moved, everything. He didn't know what form of insanity drove him to obsess about another man's wife, but his dreams of her were the only memories he had. The only thing he could hang onto.

Again, she stopped in the doorway.

Yesterday, she'd looked frightened, horrified, but today her eyes burned with anger. As if she knew about his dreams and hated him for them.

But how could she possibly know?

"If I'm such a monster to look at, maybe I should see myself," he said.

To his surprise, she laughed. "Not so much a monster as an alien. It's the green skin," she said, pulling out a mirror. She approached the bed and held it out to him. There was still some stiffness in her stance, but she didn't pull away when his fingers brushed hers as he took the mirror from her.

The pull of her gaze kept his eyes on her instead of the mirror. He wanted to drink in the sight of her, like his life depended on it, not just fodder to fuel his night-time fantasies of her.

"You don't remember me, do you?" she asked.

He blinked. Should he remember her? Outside his most recent dreams, of course. He wasn't sure.

"From before you were on the *Magellan*, I mean," she added, as if more information might help.

Her husband had been on the *Magellan*, he remembered. Stars, had he known the man? Worse, had he known her? Did that mean his dreams weren't the figments of an overactive imagination, but memories from his past – past dreams, if not reality?

What kind of monster lusted after his colleague's wife?

He glanced at the mirror, meeting the eyes of a man he didn't know. It was an inoffensive face, to be sure, and no more disfigured than the next man. Yes, his face was a brighter shade of green than his hands, but he had vague memories of someone saying that would wear off eventually. He didn't look like a monster, which probably made it worse. He handed the mirror back to her. "I'm sorry," he said.

She swallowed. "It's not your fault. Here, maybe this will help." She tucked the mirror away and pulled out her tablet, swiping across the screen until a picture appeared. "It's my favourite picture of you. I took it on the way to Titan. We were laughing so hard I'm surprised I could hold the camera still enough to take the shot."

He tilted his head to see the picture clearly. It was a photo of the man in the mirror, poised in mid air, as if surfing Saturn's rings outside the wide window. He might not recognise the man, but he knew the look in his eyes intimately. The man in the picture definitely dreamed about the photographer naked.

Stars, how long had he lusted after this woman? Did she know? Did her husband?

"What about your husband? Shouldn't

you be with him, instead of showing me old pictures?" he asked.

Anything to get her out of the room and away from him.

She pressed her lips together and tucked her tablet back into her bag, before she sat down on the chair beside his bed. "I'm here to see you," she said, a stubborn set to her jaw. "The man I married…I mourned him for four years. I never really expected him to turn up, but now...well, at least I know what happened to him."

His heart leaped in a joy so alien, he barely recognised it for what it was at first.

Stars, she'd just been widowed and here he was, being an insensitive prick and rejoicing over it? Even more of a monster. "I'm sorry for your loss," he lied. If her husband had been his friend, and he could remember him, maybe he'd have actually missed the man. Then again, if he'd loved her from afar for so long, maybe he'd have been celebrating inside, too.

"Thank you," she said evenly. "But I didn't come here to talk about mourning the man I loved, or what I should or should not be doing. I came here straight from work to see you."

Which meant she wanted to be distracted from her grief, not reminded.

He racked his brain for something to ask her about, something that might actually distract her, if only for a little while.

All he could think of was work. Not

the best thing to talk about, but it was the best he had. "How are your birds?" he asked.

She beamed. "You do remember something!"

No, he couldn't lie to her about this. He might be a monster, but he wasn't that much of a monster. "I…remember you talking about birds when I was still in the tank. Something about emus…?"

"Oh, you should see the size of the flock we have here. They're ready to send to Elysium the moment the Senate give the go ahead, but for now, they're in their own biome. I can't wait to introduce you to Darth Vader, the best dad in the galaxy…"

Entranced, he didn't question his good fortune as he just sat back and listened.

SIXTEEN

Anna wasn't sure how long she'd been talking before she realised his eyes had glazed over. Stars, he was fresh out of a regeneration tank, still recovering from injuries that nearly killed him. And here she was, boring him to tears with her birds, when she was supposed to be helping him regain his memories.

Regaling him with tales of Darth and his brood wasn't the way to go about it.

"I'm sorry," she said.

He blinked, then shook his head. "No, I'm sorry. Letting my thoughts drift away like that, when you need someone to listen."

"The hardest part about everything has been how much I just want someone to comfort me, to be there for me, and not even having that because…" You were gone, was what she wanted to say, but she couldn't, because here he was…and yet, he wasn't. It damn near did her head in.

He nodded slowly, then opened his arms. "Well, for what it's worth…"

Anna didn't hesitate. She threw herself into his embrace and for a moment, it was everything she'd been missing. All through the war, and all the years after, she'd wanted nothing more than to feel this man's arms around her again. Well, maybe a little more…

She lifted her head, more force of habit than anything else, and pressed her lips to his. The touch of his tongue was like coming home.

Someone moaned and she was embarrassed to realise it was her. Not that she could stop. This was Valentine, lost for four years, on top of the time he'd been off fighting in the war, and even if he didn't know himself, she knew him and this, THIS, was why she'd never leave him, not until she took her last breath…

"My sweet rose…" he breathed.

She stiffened. "What did you just say?" She couldn't have heard him right. He didn't recognise her, didn't know who she was, so he couldn't possibly remember…

Gently, he pushed her away from him. "I'm sorry," he said. "This is hardly the time or the place."

She rubbed her lips, swollen from his passionate kisses. Oh, for more of those kisses, but he was right. "No, but I don't regret it. After all the years, all we've lost…don't we deserve a little happiness? At least we still have each other."

A shadow passed across his face as he nodded. He was tired, she realised, and making out in his hospital bed was not going to help him recover.

"I should go. I'll see you tomorrow?"

He nodded again.

Reluctantly, she left the room, but she felt like she was floating all the way home.

SEVENTEEN

That night he dreamed about running naked in the desert again, but with her. Her breasts bouncing in the light gravity as she ran around with a light rebreather mask on her face. Then they'd made love in the red desert sands, the sunset glowing blue above them. No wonder they'd gotten sunburned.

After a dream that good, he didn't want to wake up, but the rattling catering cart with his nutrient soup was hard to ignore. But when he looked at his plate this time, he found two ration bars instead of the soup. A tiny improvement, but still better than soup.

He peeled away the wrapper and bit into one. If he chewed and swallowed it quickly, he could almost convince himself it was a chocolate bar, instead of mostly protein. Not that he could remember the last time he'd eaten chocolate.

A sudden vision of licking melted chocolate off the bird woman's breasts popped into his head. Stars, he wanted it to be a memory and not just wishful thinking. Maybe one day, when she was done mourning her husband, she might consider…

"She's a remarkable woman, your wife," a strange voice said.

He turned, only now noticing the woman who'd been sitting in a chair in the corner of his room, the tablet bearing his medical records in her hand. Fear sent his heart racing.

He knew her, he realised. Whoever she was, she held some sort of power over him.

Wait…he had a wife? If he did, and she knew how he felt about the bird woman, that might be something to fear.

"I don't…" he began.

"You talked about her so much, every time you came in for a checkup or needed some minor injury patched up, I wondered if she could be real, or even half as amazing as your stories made her out to be. But now I've met her, I finally understand. Well, I didn't actually meet her. More like stood outside Dr Calmana's office while she gave her a talking to, but it was enough to tell me everything I need to know. You are a lucky man."

Why did he think the next words out of her mouth would be threatening? What did she know about him that he didn't?

To be fair, it could be almost anything.

"What do you want from me?" he demanded. If she threatened the bird woman, he fully intended to defend her.

Her eyes widened. "Oh, I'm not here to ask you for anything. Quite the opposite, actually. I'm the messenger, now your doctor thinks you're recovered enough to hear the details of what happened to land you in her regeneration tank. You need to know a little more about your past, so you can make decisions about your future." She leaned forward, offering her hand. "I'm Maia, by the way, in case you don't remember. I was your medic aboard the *Magellan*."

"Tell me everything," he demanded.

She sat back in her seat. "Well, it was about four years ago. The *Magellan* was manoeuvring through the asteroid belt, marking suitable asteroids we could use to replenish our supplies. Water, fuel, I don't know the full list of what the ship was looking for, but from what I can gather from the stories told by the rest of the crew, someone spotted an anomaly deeper inside the asteroid belt, and the captain decided to go in to investigate. We haven't found the captain yet, but there's still hope.

"Anyway, the ship started taking fire, so we were all summoned to battle stations. You were in the medbay with me for a checkup on that dodgy heart of yours — fixed, now, after Dr Calmana grew you a whole new one, you'll be happy to hear — when the alarm went off. You headed back to the engine room, where you worked as a technician on the fusion reactor, an old model that you assured me was one bolt away from falling apart or blowing us all into stardust, and I made sure the medbay was ready for casualties, just in case.

"Now, as I imagine you already know or have guessed, the *Magellan* didn't make it, but the captain gave the order to abandon ship with enough time for most of us to make it to escape pods.

"Not you, though. According to Baris, the other engine technician working with you on that shift, the reactor had to be shut down, or it would overload and destroy the ship, and all the escape pods, too. While the alarm blared, the two of you stayed behind to shut down the reactor. Baris remembered being knocked out, before he woke up in his escape pod. He swore you must have saved his life, before shutting down the engine yourself."

Baris. Was that the bird woman's husband? "Where is Baris now?" he asked eagerly.

Maia looked blank for a moment, then consulted her tablet. "I believe he and his wife took a hobby farm in the Ag Dome. Growing fruit trees of some sort. Perfect for their two kids, twin boys, into everything. I guess I have that to look forward to when my son's older."

His heart did a sort of flip, like it wasn't sure whether to sink or soar. "Baris is alive?"

"Sure. He was one of the first to wake up. He only had minor injuries, so after a night in hospital, we sent him home with his wife, who put him straight to work. Some of the staff here are already placing bets on how soon we'll see her here in the birthing suite. You wait, she'll have enough kids to field a full football team, or at least enough to run that orchard. Definitely a breeder."

Relief flooded through him. She couldn't be the bird woman. Not if her husband was still alive and she had trees, not birds. And no mother he'd ever met could stay silent on the subject of her kids.

"Anyway, back to you. You made it to a pod, like almost everyone else on the *Magellan*. And that's it for the next four years, as you all drifted around in the asteroid belt. Now, some pods, like Baris's, were just floating in space, waiting to be picked up. Others weren't so lucky. Some got smashed open by debris from the *Magellan*. Others ran afoul of asteroids. You…got the best of both worlds. Your pod got sandwiched between a piece of debris and an asteroid, which meant your pod got damaged, but it was still mostly sealed. The impact reduced the stasis field, though, so it only protected part of your body. The other parts…were exposed to vacuum."

He winced. What they'd found can't have been pretty. It was a wonder he'd survived at all.

"Anyway, a mining crew managed the salvage. They stumbled across the *Magellan*'s debris field, and then they began to find escape pods. They called us for help, and the Colony sent out a search and rescue team to assist with salvaging the pods.

"The ice asteroid melted and refroze around your pod, protecting it until we could get you to the Colony. Getting you out of the pod and working out how much of your body could be salvaged and how much it could be regenerated…well, I understand Dr Calmana's team worked miracles over several months to bring you back. You were quite lucky, really. If your pod hadn't been damaged, you might have ended up kidnapped for some crazy alien breeding experiment." She laughed, but it had an edge to it.

Had the Titans truly…? He wasn't sure he wanted to know. If the Titans had resorted to experimenting on Human captives, they definitely deserved to lose the war.

"What about the war? Who's winning?" he asked.

Maia sighed. "I suppose we all did, in a way. The war is over. We split the system evenly between Humans and Titans, with a treaty and a Senate made up of both races to govern us all. The exception is the Colony, a dome city here on New Hope, the seventh and neutral planet in the system. It's probably the only completely civilised place in the whole Altan system, until the other planets get terraformed, which could take decades. The Colony is a little over a year old now, and still working out the kinks. That's where the future comes in, and the choice you'll have to make. It's not an easy one, I admit. It wasn't for me when I arrived here a few months ago. If it hadn't been for Ghost, I might be facing a very different future to the one I chose, or maybe even none at all. As it is, I'm happy to be here in the Colony, but you may think differently. The Colony is a mixed race city, with both Titans and Humans living in close proximity. Something you should really discuss with your wife. Whether you want to bring your kids up here, or planetside, where you can live in the open air instead of under a dome."

"I don't have a – " he began.

"Right, you don't have kids yet, but once you and your wife get settled somewhere, it's amazing how fast they come along. Some days, I can barely believe I have a son."

She'd only been here a few months and she already had a son? He wanted to ask how that was even possible, but something in her expression told him it wasn't worth his life to ask.

Maia held up her hands. "I know it's a lot to take in. You don't need to decide today, or even this week, as I know Dr Calmana would like you to stay in the Colony for at least a few more weeks, just to make sure you make a full recovery. It's not often she regenerates a patient from next to nothing, so she's going to be protective of you for a while yet. Just saying, that's something to consider if you choose to stay in the Colony. Then again, I know your wife is very serious about her work in Eden, or so I've heard.

"I know I'm not supposed to influence you one way or the other, but I'd like it if you choose to stay here in the Colony.

I'd like to get to properly meet your wife, because I think we'll get along well together. I'd love to have you both over for dinner. Oh, and if you get sick of ration bars, I can promise to only serve you real food – but I can't tell you where it came from, or I'll have to kill you."

She winked. "Only kidding. Calmana would have a conniption if I laid a hand on you, her miracle patient and all. If your wife didn't get to me first. You're a lucky man, Valentine."

He sucked in a breath, saying the name in his head. Valentine? His parents had called him Valentine? "That's my name?" he blurted out before he could think how stupid he sounded, having to ask.

Maia only laughed merrily. "Indeed it is. Valentine Gulis, the hero who stayed back and saved everyone on the *Magellan*, including Baris, besotted husband to the formidable Dr Anna Gulis, ornithologist extraordinaire, who I have no doubt will spend the rest of her life seeding emus among the stars."

Anna. The bird woman's name was Anna. Like a sigh sent straight up to heaven, it just rolled off the tongue. Anna.

Wait, had Maia said Anna was his wife? That couldn't be right.

"Maia, wait!" he called, but it was too late. While he was lost in thought, the medic had already left.

Surely Maia had it wrong. Anna couldn't be his wife…could she?

Could she?

That would mean he wasn't quite the

monster he thought he was, lusting after his colleague's wife and widow. Could he have been lusting after his own wife all this time?

Stars, how could he have been so stupid?

EIGHTEEN

When Anna entered Valentine's room, she found him sitting on a chair in the corner, instead of in the bed, and he wore a set of labourer's overalls instead of a hospital gown. He even rose to greet her.

Anna nearly cried. He looked so much like the husband she'd lost, she could almost believe it was him. But all she could say was, "You look well."

He bowed his head. "Yes, well, but I feel terrible. I owe you an apology." Before she could respond, he continued, "I've been unforgivably rude. I admit I've been pretty much stumbling in the dark, putting two and two together and getting seventeen, but it's still no excuse. Will you give me a chance to start over?"

Now she couldn't help it — she burst into tears, but they were happy ones. "That's almost exactly what you said the day we met, before you asked me out on our first date."

He squeezed his eyes shut, as if her words had hurt him. "I wish I could remember. I'm sorry I can't."

"It's all right." The words were out of

her mouth before she'd had time to think, but that didn't make them any less true.

"I take it you gave me a second chance then, and now I'm on my third at the least…okay, let's face it, if this week is any indication, I'm probably up to chance number a hundred and thirty-three…"

Anna smiled through her tears. "A thousand and thirty-three."

He whistled. "That bad, huh? How have you not divorced me yet?"

"Well, I did think you were dead for the last four years."

"You could have found someone else. Such a beautiful woman, surely you've had offers."

"None I wanted to accept. I never

could let you go. For four years, I've been working on our dream. Sending emus into space, giving them a whole new world. Just like we said we would."

Doubt creased his forehead. "I wanted more emus in the galaxy? I'm sure that can't be right. Those birds are bloody scary. A world full of them…now there's a horror movie in the making."

She laughed. "Stick with me and you'll be fine."

"One day, maybe, but I don't think I'm ready for emus yet. Maybe we'll start small, with kiwis or something."

Anna laughed. Kiwis were far more aggressive than emus, despite their small size. Not to mention territorial…they'd have to build much bigger biomes if they wanted to breed kiwis. Besides, the moa came first. "If you like," she said.

He cleared his throat. "Right. Well. If, by some miracle, you're willing to give me another chance…"

"I am."

"Then I would like to introduce myself. I am, I have recently discovered, thanks to the *Magellan*'s former medic, a fusion power technician by the name of Valentine Gulis. I have no memory of any of this, but I believe it to be the truth. I also believe you are the most beautiful, beguiling woman I have ever seen…"

Anna couldn't help laughing. "How many women do you remember seeing?"

Valentine thought for a moment. "Three. No, wait…four."

"Including me?"

"Yes. Including you."

"Hmm, that's such a small sample size, I'm not sure it could be considered statistically significant."

Valentine frowned. "Are you going to give me a chance, or just a hard time? I'm trying to ask you out on a date here."

Anna lifted her hands in surrender. "Please, proceed."

"Right. I, Valentine, would like to ask you…uh…would you believe we haven't been introduced?"

Anna wet her lips. "How…rude of me. I'm Anna. Dr Anna Gulis, ratite ornithologist at Eden Labs, and former widow of Valentine Gulis, presumed dead when the *Magellan* was lost during the war."

Valentine's eyes pinned hers and she

couldn't look away. "Please, for the amnesia patient at the back who's so hard of thinking it didn't click until yesterday…is it true that I am the husband you lost, then mourned for four years before you found out something of me survived?"

Anna took a deep breath, then blew it out again. She reached for Valentine's hands, then nearly cried when his hands engulfed hers. "You look like him. You talk like him. I'm told you even have his DNA. I don't know if you're the same man as the one I married, because you don't have all of his memories, though you might one day. But you are my husband, and I would very much like to see if I can love the man you have become as much as I loved the man you were."

He sat back, looking stunned. "Wow. I didn't dare raise my hopes above a date, and here you are, offering…wow."

Anna felt her cheeks redden. This was Valentine, and yet he wasn't. Oh, this was going to be so confusing. "A date sounds like a great start."

"Dinner, then? Where does a courting couple go on a first date, when the man's trying desperately to impress her?"

Anna smiled. "Forge, for sure. Oh, you'll love it."

NINETEEN

Perhaps she'd had a glass or two too much fizz with dinner. But the bartender had given them the bottle on the house, in honour of their special celebration, as if she'd known exactly why they were there, and Valentine wasn't supposed to drink too much alcohol, doctor's orders and all, so if she hadn't drunk it, it would have gone to waste, and it wasn't like she'd been drinking on an empty stomach, because the food at Forge was some of the best in the Colony and…stars, but it felt good when Valentine kissed her neck. She could hardly concentrate on palming open the door of her apartment, and she needed to get the door open…

A whoosh let her know she'd succeeded.

"Anna, thank you for the most wonderful night I can remember having since…well, ever, actually. Now I've seen you safely home, if you'll let me, I'd like to give you a goodnight kiss, before heading home myself…"

He'd done this on their first date, too. Some sort of archaic chivalry he'd learned on Mars.

"No. I want you to come to bed with me. Do you know how many years I've been wishing and waiting for this?"

"Actually, no, but…"

She peered up at him. "Do you want to get naked with me?"

"Well, yes, but…this is supposed to be a first date, or at least it is for me, and I'm trying to make a good impression after how horrible…"

"After our first date, we had sex three times. Four, if you count the oral in the back of the cab. Six if you count the mess we made on your breakfast table and then in the shower afterwards…"

He closed his eyes. "Stars, was that when you sat in that plate of maple syrup? You tasted so sweet I didn't want to stop…"

"You dropped to your knees, pulled my legs up over your shoulders, and made me scream so loud the neighbour came knocking on the door."

Valentine opened his eyes and they burned with desire, just like they always had. "All I remember is you."

Anna swallowed. "All I want is you. Please, Valentine."

In one swift move, he spun them into her apartment, and the door closed behind them. He barely gave the apartment a glance before he had her pinned to the wall, searing her lips with kisses. "If I make love to you six times tonight, will you forgive me for leaving you, or for my awful behaviour this week?"

He'd managed to get her shirt off, and the moment her bra followed it he fastened his mouth on her nipple, setting her on fire.

"Make love to me tonight, and I'll give you anything. Anything," she moaned.

His hand slid into her pants and between her legs…no, wait, her pants were gone, too. Like magic, except this was all Valentine. Oh, YES…

She had to wait until the stars faded from her vision before she could see his grinning face clearly enough to kiss him again. Her throat felt raw, so she must have screamed. Completely lost control…

"You're so beautiful. More beautiful than I ever dreamed. Dreams. Memories. Whatever they are, they're overrated, now I'm here with the real thing. It's like I'm seeing you for the first time, but I know exactly what you like…"

His hand slid between her legs again, his eyes never leaving hers. A few strokes had her breathless. A little more pressure as he built up speed made her moan his name. Then he slipped a third finger inside her, hooking it just right, and all Anna could do was scream for joy.

"Make love to me, Valentine! Please!" she implored. "I'll do anything. Give you anything. I've waited so long…"

"Anything?" he asked, teasing her nipple again.

"Anything," she swore.

"Here or on the bed?"

"Valentine, please!"

He carried her to the bed, setting her

down right in the middle so she could watch him strip off. He was harder than she remembered. More muscle. She couldn't deny that she liked it. Arms that could lift her effortlessly. Ridges that ran right down his belly, pointing towards the bulge in his shorts, the only clothing he still wore.

"Please," she whispered.

"Not before I've tasted you, my sweet rose."

It was the most arousing thing any man had ever said to her, and it took her right back to that first maple syrup morning.

Valentine knelt between her thighs, lifting her spread legs onto his shoulders before he leaned forward. The heat of his breath teased her, making her wish she could open herself wider, so he could reach more of her. "My sweet, full blown rose," he whispered as his fingers speared her, before he went to work with his tongue. Ever so slowly, he stroked and swirled, every caress as soft as a rose petal. No matter how much she begged him to go faster, harder, he kept up the same maddeningly light pace. Yet every stroke brought her closer and closer to a peak only Valentine could make her reach.

She could feel it now, like dangling over the edge of a precipice, with only Valentine keeping her from toppling over. One little push…

"Please, Valentine," she begged.

He let out a breathy laugh, the warmth of it almost enough to send her flying.

Almost.

She held her breath. Had he remembered? Was he going to? Oh, please…

He sealed her fate with a kiss, so that all at once, she was screaming, soaring, clenching, sucking in a breath, then screaming again.

How many years had she waited for this climax? They were all worth it, all worth it, even if it was only once. The first time he'd done it, he'd nearly blown her mind, and now…

Now he was laughing at her, the brute who looked and sounded like her husband. "Stars, Anna, I'm tempted to do that all over again, just to hear you scream my name like that again."

"Yes. Please. A dozen times. A

thousand times yes. I'm yours, Valentine."

He chuckled as he let her legs slide back down to the bed. "Maybe in the morning. And again tomorrow night. And the next morning."

"Yes," she breathed. What else had he remembered? Was he going to…?

He rolled onto his back on the bed beside her, then slid his shorts off.

Stars, she'd forgotten how big he was. How she'd ached after that first night. How she'd ached with need for him so many nights since.

"Are you ready for me, my sweet rose?" he whispered.

Yes. No. Yes.

She straddled him, hissing as his heat seared the already sensitive skin he'd rubbed so relentlessly. Now it was her turn to be slow, sinking down on him to let her body grow accustomed to his girth. How could she have forgotten this feeling of fullness? And when he moved within her…oh, stars…no one touched her quite as deeply as he did.

"Anna, are you all right? Am I hurting you?"

She shook her head, unable to find the words.

"You're crying, Anna. Please, talk to me. What's wrong?"

She stared down into his worried eyes, tears blurring her vision. "Nothing's wrong. As long as I have you, nothing will ever be wrong again." She rocked her hips against him, groaned at how good it felt, then did it again. And again.

She couldn't bear to stop, it felt so incredible. So incredible she was going to…no, she couldn't already…oh yes…yes she could…

"I love you, Valentine!" she screamed as her vision went white.

An eternity later, she managed to focus on his face again. He'd wrapped his hands around her hips, guiding her as he matched her rhythm. "We're going to come together this time, Anna," he said.

Words had left her again. All she could do was nod as she rocked against him, the movement almost hypnotic. There was nothing in the universe but the two of them, and the heat building inside her. His heat. Her heat. No, definitely his heat. But she was about to explode…

"Together," Valentine said, breathing

hard as he drove up into her. "Always."

"Yes," she breathed. "Yes, yes, YES!"

When she blinked away the stars obscuring her vision, she found herself lying on his chest, surprised to realise he'd already cleaned up. She'd never missed that particular chore before.

"So how do I measure up?" he asked.

Enormous, she thought, until he laughed, as if she'd said it aloud. Maybe she had.

"I mean compared to the man you were married to before," he said. "Do I deserve a second date?"

She pretended to consider the question, though there was only one answer in her mind. "That depends. Do you believe in sex on a second date?"

He chuckled. "I believe I'd like to go

straight to the sex and skip the date. But the choice is yours, Anna."

She smiled. "That's not what you said the first time. You took me to some new restaurant you swore your friends had raved about. We both got food poisoning, so there wasn't any sex. Not for a whole week."

"That…is one memory I'm glad I don't have. Sounds awful. Did you ever forgive me?"

"Maybe." She looked up at him. Stars, but she'd missed him. He might not remember everything, but he was still her Valentine. She'd forgive him anything – he only had to ask.

He slipped a hand between her legs, stroking. "What do I have to do to earn a second date?"

Anna gasped, which only made him stroke harder.

"Please, Anna," he whispered, but she couldn't focus on anything but his fingers, circling and swirling. She couldn't possibly…could she?

"Valentine…stars, Valentine!" she tried to shout, but it only came out as a hoarse whisper. And his fingers hadn't stopped. She'd barely descended from the first peak and he had her climbing again. Not…possible… "Oh, Valentine!"

He licked his fingers slowly, savouring the taste. "You're still my sweet rose. Six orgasms on the first date earned me that disastrous second date, you said. So, when are you willing to let me take you on a second date that will make you forget the other man?"

There was no other man. Valentine was the only man for her, forever and always. "Whenever you want," she said dreamily, gazing up at him.

He grinned. "How about now, then? We can skip straight to the sex."

He rolled them, so he was on top, before shifting to kneel between her legs. He lifted her legs up onto his shoulders, sliding a pillow under her to raise her hips.

"Just say the word, Anna," he said, already poised to enter her.

"YES!"

ABOUT THE AUTHOR

Demelza Carlton has always loved the ocean, but on her first snorkelling trip she found she was afraid of fish.

She has since swum with sea lions, sharks and sea cucumbers and stood on spray drenched cliffs over a seething sea as a seven-metre cyclonic swell surged in, shattering a shipwreck below.

Demelza now lives in Perth, Western Australia, the shark attack capital of the world.

The *Ocean's Gift* series was her first foray into fiction, followed by her suspense thriller *Nightmares* trilogy. She swears the *Mel Goes to Hell* series ambushed her on a crowded train and wouldn't leave her alone.

Want to know more? You can follow Demelza on Facebook, Twitter, YouTube or her website, Demelza Carlton's Place at:

www.demelzacarlton.com

More Books by Demelza Carlton

<u>Colony: Holiday series</u>

Cowboys and Aliens (#1)

Ghost (#2)

Vulcan (#3)

Cupid (#4)

Valentine(#5)

Prometheus (#6)

<u>**Colony: Aqua series**</u>

Halcyon (#1)

Poseidon (#2)

Apollo (#3)

<u>**Siren of Secrets series**</u>

Ocean's Secret (#1)

Ocean's Gift (#2)

Ocean's Infiltrator (#3)

<u>**Nightmares Trilogy**</u>

Nightmares of Caitlin Lockyer (#1)

Necessary Evil of Nathan Miller (#2)

Afterlife of Alana Miller (#3)

<u>Romance Island Resort series</u>

Maid for the Rock Star (#1)

The Rock Star's Email Order Bride (#2)

The Rock Star's Virginity (#3)

The Rock Star and the Billionaire (#4)

The Rock Star Wants A Wife (#5)

The Rock Star's Wedding (#6)

Maid for the South Pole (#7)

<u>Romance a Medieval Fairytale series</u>

Enchant: Beauty and the Beast Retold

Dance: Cinderella Retold

Fly: Goose Girl Retold

Revel: Twelve Dancing Princesses Retold

Silence: Little Mermaid Retold

Awaken: Sleeping Beauty Retold

Embellish: Brave Little Tailor Retold

Appease: Princess and the Pea Retold

Blow: Three Little Pigs Retold

Return: Hansel and Gretel Retold

Wish: Aladdin Retold

Melt: Snow Queen Retold

Spin: Rumpelstiltskin Retold

Kiss: Frog Prince Retold

Reflect: Snow White Retold

Roar: Goldilocks Retold

Cobble: Elves and the Shoemaker Retold

Float: Enchanted Horse Retold

Steal: Forty Thieves Retold

Call: Pied Piper Retold

Fall: Scheherazade Retold

Feather: Swan Maidens Retold

Cross: Billy Goats Gruff Retold

Weave: Rapunzel Retold

Claim: Puss in Boots Retold

Curse: Rose Red Retold

www.ingramcontent.com/pod-product-compliance
Lightning Source LLC
Chambersburg PA
CBHW071000180726
48291CB00004B/1379